This igloo book belongs to:

....

igloobooks

Published in 2013
by Igloo Books Ltd
Cottage Farm
Sywell
NN6 0BJ
www.igloobooks.com

FIR003 1013
4 6 8 10 9 7 5 3
ISBN: 978-1-78197-298-4

Printed and manufactured in China

I Love you Mummy

igloobooks

I love you, Mummy,
because you cover me with kisses,
like warm sunbeams when I wake.

When we play hide-and-seek and I peek,
you say, "Boo! Found you,"
and you tickle me until I giggle.

Mummy, I love you because
when I tumble into muddy puddles, you
wash me and then make me warm and dry.

When I am scared, you are there to
hold out your arms and keep
me from harm and catch me when I fall.

I love you, Mummy, because you smell like summer flowers and are soft and snuggly like a bed made of feathers.

When snowy weather comes, you keep
me cozy and warm and we count
snowflakes falling from the sky.

Mummy, I love you because
you play with me all day and give me
hugs and treats and nice things to eat.

When the sun is low,
I sit on your lap and you rock and pat my
back and hum like happy honey bees.

I love you, Mummy, because you
show me the stars and the bright, round moon
and whisper to me, gently,
"Hush, now, shush now, settle down."

I love you, Mummy, because
you hold me close, as I drift off to sleep
and dream of how much you love me.

I love you, Mummy, because
you're *my* mummy.